Wiggler's Worms

Stories about God's Green Earth

Paulette Nehemias

Illustrated by Jim Harris

CONCORDIA

PUBLISHING HOUSE

Stories about God's Green Earth

A Tree in Sprocket's Pocket
Wiggler's Worms

Wiggler's Worms
is printed on recycled paper.

Copyright © 1993 Concordia Publishing House
3558 S. Jefferson Avenue, St. Louis, MO 63118-3968
Manufactured in the United States of America

Library of Congress Cataloging-in-Publication Data

Nehemias, Paulette, 1958-
    Wiggler's worms: stories about God's green earth / Paulette Nehemias; illustrated by Jim Harris.
(God's green earth; bk.)
    Summary: A collection of short stories with accompanying activities which raise children's environmental awareness and describe ways to help care for God's earth.
    ISBN 0-570-04731-5
    1. Children's stories , American. [1. Environmental protection—Fiction. 2. Ecology—Fiction. 3. Christian life—Fiction. 4. Short stories.] I. Harris, Jim, 1955— ill. II. Title. III. Series
PZ7. N423W1 1993
[Fic]—dc20   92-28486
                                                            CIP

1 2 3 4 5 6 7 8 9 10   02 01 00 99 98 97 96 95 94 93

Contents

Wiggler's Worms

Jason rushed into class with a note for his all-time favorite Sunday school teacher.

"Here, Pastor Olsen. Mayor Brown met me at the door and asked me to give this to you."

Pastor Olsen took the note, and Jason wiggled in his seat as he waited for the pastor to finish reading. As Pastor Olsen folded up the note, he chuckled, "Oh, that Wiggler. He always comes through for us . . . "

"Who's Wiggler?" Jason asked, before he even thought about whether it was his business to know. But the pastor didn't seem to notice. He smiled as he took the time to consider Jason's question.

Of all the adults he knew, Jason felt most comfortable with Pastor Olsen. Pastor Olsen never called Jason "hyperactive."

"Everybody in town likes Mayor Brown," Jason added. "Is that who Wiggler is? I'm sure glad he got elected. But why is he always in such a hurry?"

Pastor thought for a moment and then decided to tell Jason a story that would answer both questions. "You know how you and I always enjoy a good fishing trip, Jason?"

Did he ever. In the small Nebraska town where they lived, there was plenty of wonderful fishing right close by. Sometimes Jason would ride his bike to the lake with a friend, and they would catch bluegills on a sunny afternoon. Sometimes his grandfather and Pastor Olsen would take Jason out very early in the morning, and they'd fish for bass before the sun came up.

"Jason, are you listening to me?" asked the story-telling pastor. He began his tale. "About 25 years ago, there was another boy in this church who loved to fish. Everyone called him

Wiggler. I'm not sure if it was because his favorite bait was wiggly worms, or if it was because he had lots of extra energy. Anyway, Wiggler went fishing absolutely every chance he got. After school, weekends, holidays, you always knew that Wiggler was somewhere near water.

"Wiggler was just enough different from the other boys in town that he didn't have much use for them, nor they for him. Oh, he was a nice boy, but he was always in a hurry or dreaming about some wild adventure. He just moved too fast for the other boys and, frankly, they bored him a little bit. Anyway, his grandfather was his favorite fishing buddy. They'd spend hours doing fishing stuff, like digging the biggest worms from the vegetable garden or tying their newest idea for the perfect trout fly. Then they'd head to the water and sit and share stories, dreams, and adventures. They were quite a pair.

"In the late summer, after Wiggler's 13th birthday, his grandfather died. Everything changed. The house, with the worm-growing vegetable garden was sold, and Wiggler wasn't quite sure just what would happen next. I had just become pastor here, and Wiggler and I did a lot of talking that fall. Wiggler had heard his grandfather talk about God often enough; he knew his grandfather loved God. But Wiggler was sad and angry that God had let his grandfather die. Wiggler needed more than just memories of his grandfather, he wanted his grandfather with him for real!

"A couple weeks before Christmas I asked Wiggler if I could take him fishing. The lakes were frozen solid. Wiggler's grandfather had never taken him ice fishing. Since I was from Minnesota, I had lots of memories of huddling in a packing crate with a small fire for heat and a hole cut in the ice for our fishing lines. I was delighted when Wiggler said he would go with me.

"After several fishing trips and lots of talking about God and love and family, Wiggler decided that his memories of his grandfather were very precious. He knew that his grandfather was with Jesus in heaven. And he knew that God still loved him.

"But on one trip, Wiggler said, `I sure miss my fishing trips with Grandpa. And where am I ever going to find worms as big and wiggly as the ones in Grandpa's garden?'

"That's when I pulled out a little book I had brought along for Wiggler. He probably thought it was a Bible at first, and maybe it should have been. But instead, it was a small book about raising your own earthworms for fishing bait and soil improvement.

"Wiggler took that book and flipped through it. Within weeks, he was devoting all his energy—which was a lot, remember?—to raising the biggest and best worms in eastern Nebraska. In a short time, Wiggler had more worms than he needed for his own fishing, so he began selling them to other anglers. With the money he made, he started raising more earthworms for all the gardeners in town. Before too long, anybody who bought a new house in town knew that the best supply of worms to improve their yard soil was available from Wiggler. Anybody who wanted to catch big fish or grow better plants was calling Wiggler for worms!"

"Wait a minute," interrupted Jason. "How do earthworms make dirt better for growing plants?"

"Good question, Jason." Pastor Olsen didn't mind the interruption. He explained that plants need to be able to get their nutrients from the soil around them. Any time the top-soil is removed, like when a new house is built, plants will have a hard time getting started. The soil isn't as nutrient rich. Or if the soil is overworked, the nutrients need to be replenished.

Worms help make soil healthier for plants in two ways. In hard-packed ground that has a lot of clay, worms can burrow through and make tunnels through the soil. That helps the roots get to the nutrients. As the worms swallow the soil, they digest it. Then the worm castings are rich in nitrogen, phosphates, and other plant delicacies—all ready for the plant to use.

Pastor Olsen finished explaining and took up Wiggler's story again. "Wiggler made enough money from his worm business to start paying for college. He studied public speaking and environmental science. He came back to town, kept working to improve our environment, and just recently won his first election."

"So, Mayor Brown is Wiggler! I mean Wiggler is Mayor Brown," laughed Jason.

"That's right. Young Wiggler put his energy to work and grew up to help God's creation and the people of our town. And this note you gave me? It says he'll be able to help out with the new organ the church needs. Good ol' Wiggler always comes through . "

Jason heard familiar noises out in the hall and realized the rest of his class was about to join them. Before they came into the room, Jason had just two more questions to ask Pastor Olsen.

"Pastor, do you have another copy of that earthworm book?" After a pause he added, "And do you think maybe you could call me Wiggler too?"

GOD'S CYCLE—A WINDOW PICTURE

Materials

- Wax paper
- Two pieces of construction paper
- Tissue or construction paper scraps
- Crayon shavings
- Iron
- Newspaper
- Markers
- Stapler or glue
- String

1. Cut identical windows from both pieces of construction paper. These will form the front and back of your picture frame.
2. Cut two pieces of wax paper slightly larger than the construction paper.
3. Lay one piece of construction paper on a thick layer of newspaper. Place one sheet of wax paper over the construction-paper "frame." Lay a piece of string on the wax paper, to serve as a fishing line. Cut or tear worm and fish shapes from paper scraps and arrange them on the wax paper.
4. Add interest to the design by dropping a few crayon shavings or bits of tissue-paper "seaweed" on the wax paper.
5. Lay the second piece of wax paper on top of your design. Cover with several sheets of newspaper and iron for about 45 seconds. Uncover and allow "picture" to cool.
6. Staple or glue on top construction-paper frame. Trim away extra wax paper. Use a marker or crayon to write sentences around the frame: Worms help soil. Soil helps plants. Plants help worms.

Running the Race

The sound of the other kids' laughter was almost drowned out as the bus doors closed, but not quite. As the bus pulled away from Brian's stop, he could still hear the teasing. The lead boy, Erik, just couldn't give it a rest. Out the back window of the bus, he was pointing a finger at redheaded 13-year-old Brian, and with the other hand he was twisting a strand of his own hair around his finger.

Brian was so mad his cheeks were as red as his hair! But it was more than just his red hair that made him the odd kid out. Brian Peterson was different from the others. He didn't fit in, and he knew it. School was boring. Too simple and too slow. Although he was a good hiker and an excellent rock climber, he wasn't a good athlete. He liked being on his own, like in chess or computer games. But unlike the computerheads at school, he just couldn't stand to be indoors day after day.

As Brian approached his house, his thoughts were interrupted by the sound of singing coming from the backyard. Brian sighed as he remembered it was Thursday. Mom would be baby-sitting three extra kids until dinnertime. His life had really turned around since Dad left. Every Monday, Wednesday, and Thursday, Mom was paid to baby-sit three kids. On Tuesday and Friday she worked in an office at the hospital.

Brian looked over the backyard gate just in time to see his mother and the four little kids finish the verse, "Ashes, ashes, we all fall down!" They all tumbled on the ground laughing. Brian rolled his eyes and shook his head. Silly games. Mom could be fairly intelligent when she and Brian were talking by themselves, but that was pretty rare. Usually Keith or the other little kids were around, and Mom would act like a real space cadet. She couldn't think about what Brian was saying, and most of the time she couldn't even listen.

Brian hung his backpack in the usual spot, a hook high up on the porch where the little kids couldn't get into it. He waved to his mom, grabbed a snack from the tray on the table, and headed for his grandfather's house.

Brian's parents had built their house on a corner of his grandparents' ranch. His grandmother had died before Brian was old enough to remember her, but Grandpa had always been there for Brian. He couldn't imagine it any other way. Grandpa was just as interested in Brian's discoveries as Brian was. And Grandpa seemed to understand about Brian being teased about his red hair. Grandpa had red hair. Well, he used to have red hair back when he had hair.

Brian could complain to Grandpa about anything. Grandpa would always listen and would somehow always end up giving the same advice: God gives each of us a race to run.

He gives us everything we need to do our best. He even let His Son die and rise again to win the race for us. With God beside us, we can't lose!

Grandpa always said that God's world was full of wonders and wasn't that wonderful. Brian was thinking about that play on words as he got to Grandpa's workshop. Grandpa wasn't there.

"Grandpa, where are you?" called Brian.

From far off in the distance came Grandpa's familiar whistle. Grandpa was just coming out of the woods. His dog, Shadrach, was dancing around at his feet. It looked like Grandpa was carrying something, but he was too far away for Brian to see what it was.

Gently Grandpa carried the bundle in his arms. Yet by the look on his face, Grandpa was furious about something. Brian jumped out of his way as Grandpa stormed to the house.

"Some idiot shot Sarah," was all he said. Brian was stunned. He hurried to catch up with his grandfather. With wide eyes he fearfully asked, "Is she . . . dead?"

Grandpa saw the look on Brian's face,

stopped, and explained. "No, she's not dead," he started, "but she's hurt pretty badly. She needs help."

Sarah was a red-tailed hawk—a female. Abraham was the male in the pair of hawks that had been nesting in the cliffs above Grandpa's woods.

Grandpa took the bundle straight into the kitchen and gently laid it on the table. Sarah didn't even move. Ever so carefully Grandpa began to unwrap the towel. Brian caught his breath when he saw spots of dark red on the tan towel. He began to fear the worst.

One long wing was fully extended. Grandpa quickly and gently folded the wing close to the bird's body. "I don't need a scared hawk flapping around my kitchen table," he explained. "She wasn't hit in either wing. That's probably good if we ever expect her to fly again."

Brian had never seen such a powerful bird up close. Although the feathers were matted with dry blood and there was still a little bleeding, Brian couldn't help but be fascinated

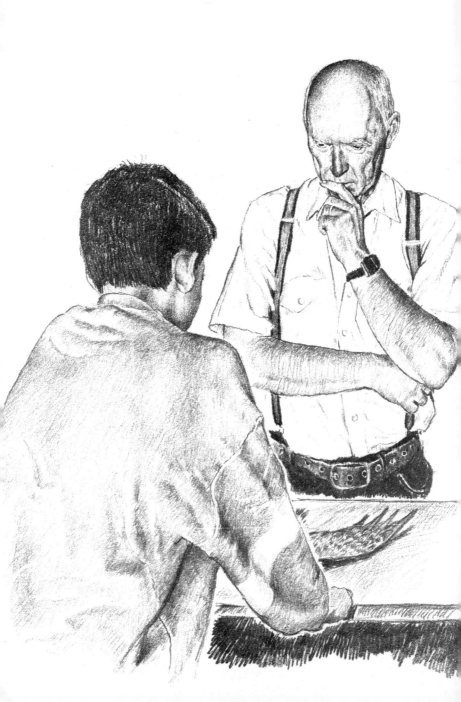

by the dangerous talons on the short, thick legs of the big bird.

"Be careful, Grandpa," he said. But Mr. Peterson needed no reminders. As he slowly turned Sarah over, the old man sighed. Even though she was limp while he examined her, Grandpa was careful to be sure that her wings were always held securely against her body. Female hawks are larger than males, and the talons are treacherous. Grandpa and Brian couldn't risk any wild wing-flapping that might distract them from Sarah's powerful legs and sharp beak. Grandpa began to wrap Sarah tightly in the towel again. Brian hadn't even seen the small bullet holes, probably because he was studying every other feature of the bird so carefully. The keen eyes, the sharp beak, the size of that wing—amazing!

"Good thing it wasn't a shotgun," Grandpa said after the bird was wrapped snugly.

"Are the bullets still in there?" wondered Brian.

"How do I know?" shrugged Grandpa. "I don't know anything about gunshot wounds."

All he could tell was that Sarah hadn't been shot with a shotgun, and that was good.

Grandpa called a nearby park. Maybe someone there could help. The ranger couldn't tell them anything, but he did give them the number of the Lindsey Museum, a nearby wildlife rehabilitation center. Grandpa called and found that the center helped more than 9,000 injured wild animals each year. That was the good news. The bad news was that Brian and his grandfather wouldn't be able to care for Sarah at home. It was against the law. They would have to bring her to the center in Walnut Creek.

"But Grandpa, she's your bird," Brian complained. But Mr. Peterson said that the folks at the Lindsey Museum would know more about nursing poor Sarah.

Brian got Shadrach's travel cage from the garage to use for the bird. Even though she was still wrapped in a towel, she began to struggle a bit. That was a good sign.

Brian and Grandpa's determination to see Sarah fly again was strong. "I hope they know what they're doing," said Brian, as they began the 30-minute drive to Walnut Creek.

"The Lindsey Museum is the oldest and largest wildlife rehabilitation center in the United States. They'll know what they're doing."

Two women in white lab coats were waiting for Sarah when Mr. Peterson's car pulled up. They quickly disappeared with Sarah behind the door of what must have been the examining room. Brian and his grandfather stood empty-handed as the swinging door swung shut. The sign on the door said "Employees Only."

Brian and Grandpa had no choice but to wander through the museum, waiting for news about Sarah. They read about trees and how they grow, fish and their spawning needs, and even about woodpeckers that make thousands of small holes in dead trees to store acorns. One hole for every acorn! Brian had never heard of such a thing. Beautiful displays! The people here really cared about God's creation. Wild things need to stay wild. That's best.

In another room the walls were lined with aquariums, snake tanks, and elaborate cages for live animals. There were a couple of rabbits, a raccoon, a fox, an opossum, a groundhog, some other rodents, and many small birds. Above the cages were perches for the big birds. Brian was thrilled to see two owls, a turkey vulture, and several hawks perched high up on the small stands. But then a guide, not much older than he, explained that these animals were really the failures of the center.

"Our goal is always to return the animals to the wild," she said. "For one reason or another, none of the animals in this room would be able to survive away from the center."

Brian thought of Sarah and felt his stomach tighten as the guide described the injuries of each bird that had caused the permanent damage. Grandpa was angry when he learned that most of these birds had been shot.

Just then one of the women came out of the animal hospital and introduced herself. Her name was Abby. She smiled and said, "The bird has not been shot in the wing. If she lives,

22

she'll be able to fly again."

"She'll live," said the old man and his grandson together.

Brian and Grandpa drove home feeling like they had done the right thing, but a little bothered that someone else was now in charge. "Grandpa, we forgot to ask about where she's going to be released! She *has* to come back to the farm. What about Abraham?"

The next morning Brian called the center. He wanted to come in after school and see how Sarah was doing. After a little hesitation, Abby said okay.

At the center Brian asked to go back into the hospital section and see Sarah. Abby warned him not to get too attached to the bird—not because she might die, but because Sarah should have as little contact with people as possible if she was to return to the wild. Grandpa waited behind, but Brian was determined to sneak a peak at Sarah. He was surprised to see her standing up. She looked alert and had a bandage wrapped around her middle.

As they left, Brian told Abby they'd be back the next morning. They'd be able to stay longer since it was Saturday.

Abby shook her head. "Only the museum staff and volunteers are allowed back here. I can't keep letting you come in like this."

"Then I'll be a volunteer!" said Brian without hesitation.

Brian's cheeks burned red hot, and he held back tears as Abby explained that the minimum age for volunteers to work with the animals was 16. The only thing that 13-year-olds could do at the museum was lead children's tours through the two exhibition rooms. Brian thought of the kids his mom took care of. No way could he be a tour guide for them. He stormed off to the car.

It was a long, quiet ride home, but Brian's mind was working. Just as they pulled in the driveway, he told Grandpa his plan.

Grandpa could be a volunteer and keep an eye on Sarah. Then Brian could ride to the center with him to see how Sarah was doing.

Grandpa thought for a minute, then decided it was an idea worth exploring. "But Brian," he explained, "if I take the orientation class and become a volunteer, I can't break any rules just to let you in the back to see Sarah."

"That won't happen," Brian assured him. "I'll stay in the display rooms."

Three afternoons a week Grandpa would pick Brian up at school, and they would drive to Walnut Creek. For two hours at a time Brian would hang out in the two rooms of the center while Grandpa worked in the back. Grandpa worked with a listless Canada goose, a raccoon that had been hit by a car, and his favorite—a noisy little woodpecker. As for Brian, he read every display over and over. After a few weeks, whenever visitors would ask questions, Brian could answer them.

Every day when Brian asked about Sarah, he got encouraging news. But the wildlife director continued to remind Brian not to get attached to Sarah. "Remember, this business is always about good-bye," she would say.

Finally the day came for Sarah's release. Abby brought her out in a carrier and rode with Brian and Grandpa back to the ranch. "Hawks are territorial birds, and Abraham is waiting for her," Abby explained.

Mom joined them out in the field, and Brian suggested Keith come along. "He may be too young to remember, but it's time he started appreciating wild things too," he said in a grown-up voice. Brian carried the cage down the path toward the woods. Up above, Abraham was soaring above the cliffs in search of food. Every so often he would call out, "Keee-eer, keee-eer."

Sarah didn't answer, but she was making quite a fuss in the closed-up carrier.

They set the carrier on a flat rock in view of Sarah's nest and her mate, and close to a stand of oak trees.

Everyone stood like stone as Brian grasped the latch on the cage door. He was so excited he could hardly keep his hands still. The latch clicked, the door opened, Brian backed away, and it seemed the whole world paused in anticipation.

After a long moment, Sarah slowly strutted through the cage door opening. She blinked once or twice, looked toward the sky, and cocked her head. Then, suddenly, she spread her wings, and with a few strong flaps, she lifted herself into the sky. She headed straight for the woods and landed in the closest tree.

After a few minutes, Sarah once again spread her wings and stepped off the branch. Down she glided—just for a moment—and then, with those powerful wings, she lifted herself higher into the sky. Higher and higher she circled, then she finally called out, "Keee-eer, keee-eer."

Abraham had been out of sight, but returned when he heard his mate's calls. They circled and called for awhile, then started flying together. They circled and dived and, at one point, they seemed to grab each other's legs and almost do cartwheels in the air.

The whole group stood in awe of the splendid sight, and no one said a word until Keith pointed up and said, "Sarah's laughing!"

Everyone was in a festive mood as they walked back to the house. Mom served refreshments.

"Tell me, Mr. Peterson," Abby asked Grandpa, "Where did you learn so much about birds?" Before Grandpa could answer, Brian got the seventh volume of Grandpa's encyclopedia. He looked up "hawk" and read to the group all the interesting facts that Grandpa had been sharing with him during their hawk-watching trips.

They all laughed. Grandpa said to Brian, "I told you that God gives us all a race to run, and He gives us everything we need to run that race. The most important part of the race is knowing Jesus as our Savior. But also I know that God wants me to help encourage your love of His creation. To do that, He gave me my good health, this old ranch—and encyclopedias! Now you can share your sense of wonder at God's creation with all you meet."

Abby thanked Mom for the refreshments. Then she turned to Brian and Grandpa. "So, I'll see you two at the museum on Monday. Brian,

I'm wondering if you would be interested in giving a tour next Thursday? What do you think?"

Brian and Grandpa exchanged smiles. There was only one answer to that question.

SPREAD THE WORD POSTER

Materials
- Sketch paper
- Pencils
- Felt-tip markers or poster paint
- Poster board
- Masking tape and/or thumbtacks

Call nature centers and state parks in the area where you live. Find out if there is a wildlife rehabilitation center near your home. Learn about the animals that are native to your area. Which animals in your area are more at risk than others? What are the causes of danger for the animals in your area? What good things are people doing for them? What are people doing that might be harmful for the animals?

Design posters that applaud good things people are doing for animals native to your area, and point out things that may be harmful to a native species.

Ask permission to put your posters up at school, in your public library, at the post office, and on other community bulletin boards. Send a poster to your newspaper with a story about the animals in your area. Send posters and copies of your story to the news departments of your area radio and TV stations.

Mother Martha

"Mom! Mom!" called Martha Cooper, "I need an empty shoebox or something. Quick!"

Pride barked excitedly, and before Mrs. Cooper could ask what for, Martha grabbed an empty potato-chip carton and headed out the back door.

Out in the yard, Martha stopped and listened for the rustling noise in the bushes. She didn't hear the sound she was hoping for, but Pride sniffed around and found the little bit of red-brown fluff snuggled in the summer-green lawn. Martha tiptoed over to the tiny animal and gently lowered the box over her patient.

"See, Mom?" Martha said to her mom, who had followed her outside. "It's a baby bird. I can't see a nest or a mother bird. It must be an orphan. Look how limp and quiet it is. I think it's a baby cardinal, but he's not bright red. Can I keep it?"

Mrs. Cooper sighed. She knew the family was leaving for a camping trip to Maine in two days. But she was worried about the helpless bird too. She called the nature center and was told that Martha could try to help the bird, but that it might be too weak to live. The first thing the bird would need would be warmth.

Mrs. Cooper hung up the phone and said, "Let's make a warm nest for it and then see if it can eat."

While Martha put a paper towel in a clean berry basket, mother got a heating pad and a tweezer. Then Mother went to look for an eyedropper.

Martha gently placed the fragile bird in its new home on top of the heating pad. After a short time in the cozy, warm basket, the little bird started to look less sad.

"Its name is Chipper," Martha announced when Mom returned with an eyedropper and a large book about birds. The book said that the first feathers of a young male cardinal were brownish red, and that the bright red feathers grew later. Yes, Chipper was a cardinal.

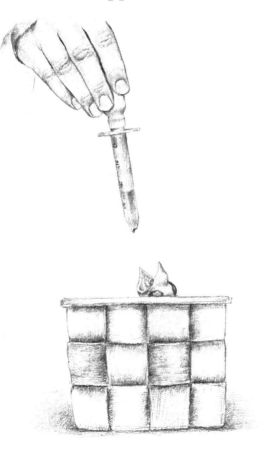

Mom read in the book that warm milk with a bit of sugar should be Chipper's first food. When the baby bird discovered the sweet treat in the eyedropper, the milk disappeared quickly. Chipper could eat just fine.

Once Chipper knew that Martha and Mrs. Cooper were gentle and kind, he started chirping loudly every time he was hungry. Martha was busy the rest of the day. If she wasn't feeding Chipper, she was mixing up the egg yolk, bread crumb, and milk mixture for his next meal.

By the time Mr. Cooper got home, Chipper was looking and acting much stronger.

"If the bird lives, Martha, what are you going to do when we go on vacation?" he asked. "Being a bird's mother is a full-time job."

Martha considered that as she got ready for bed. She was sure everything would work out with the trip and all, but she was more worried about the number of times she would need to get up and feed Chipper during the night. Mom said she would tend to the baby while Martha slept.

Martha tucked Chipper in and said goodnight to her parents. Just before she fell asleep with her arm around Pride, she whispered, "Thanks, God, for letting me find Chipper today. Please help Chipper live and be happy."

Two days later Chipper was very much alive. As the Coopers began loading the trailer for their trip, Martha scurried around to gather up all the things she would need to take care of Chipper while they were gone. Mr. Cooper laughed, "I see there's no separating Martha from her new baby, and I'd rather take the bird to Maine than leave Martha home in Maryland!"

By now Chipper was very perky. Martha still had to feed him by hand, but when he wasn't eating or sleeping he chirped happily. Because of all the hand-feeding, Chipper was tame and affectionate. He perched on Martha's finger and hopped up her arm. When he sat on her shoulder, he nibbled her brown hair and gave her ear little bird kisses. Martha laughed and scratched Chipper under his beak.

Chipper could hop out of his berry basket now by himself. Martha kept the nest in a big box, so Chipper could move around or rest whenever he wanted. But that box would be too big for the drive in the car. Martha found a bushel basket with a screen lid for Chipper.

Finally everything was packed. Mr. and Mrs. Cooper sat in the front seat, and Martha rode in the back with Chipper and Pride. Martha was sure this was going to be the best vacation ever.

The trip seemed to make Chipper nervous. He danced around, chirping in a funny way, as if he was calling Martha. Since Chipper couldn't see out of the bushel basket, he didn't know that Martha was right next to him. She spoke gently to the bird, and he settled down a bit.

After they'd been driving a long while, Mr. Cooper thought it would be okay to take Chipper out of the basket. Chipper was perfectly content to perch on Martha's shoulder for hours at a time. Martha made sure Chipper was sitting on her shoulder as cars passed so that other people could see as they drove by. She was very proud of her little cardinal.

The only time Chipper went back into his bushel basket cage was when the car windows or doors had to be opened. After toll booths and gas station stops Chipper came back out of his cage, hopped right up to Martha's shoulder, and snuggled down for the next few hours.

Chipper ate practically anything these days, but his favorites were sunflower seeds, peanut butter, and bits of fruit. He didn't know it yet, but he was in for a real treat when he would taste fresh Maine blueberries! And baths? Chipper loved to take baths. Martha discovered this in the trailer one evening after dinner.

While Martha and Mom were washing dishes, Chipper sat on Martha's shoulder. Chipper hopped down onto the sink. He must have been curious about the soap bubbles because he reached out to them with his beak. Pride barked suddenly, and—splash!—Chipper fell in the water. Quickly, Mrs. Cooper scooped him out of the water, but he was already wet. Since Martha knew birds could die from colds, she looked around for a way to dry Chipper. But Chipper already had an answer. He hopped over to a small lamp and perched himself on the lampshade. There he fluffed his feathers out, then shook himself all over, just like Pride did after a swim.

Chipper's fluffed-out feathers made him look about twice as fat as he really was. He stayed there and preened himself until every feather was dry and back in place. Then he fell asleep.

Mrs. Cooper gave Martha a clean lid from a peanut butter jar. Every night she put some warm water in it for Chipper's bath. Chipper splashed about for awhile and then headed to the nearest lamp to perch and preen until he fell asleep.

When the Coopers went sightseeing in New England, they left Chipper in his cage back in the trailer. After going out for some Maine lobster one night, Martha and her parents were surprised to see a small crowd of people and a park ranger gathered near the window of their locked trailer. Sure that something had happened to Chipper, they ran to the trailer.

"It's the strangest thing," said the ranger. "There's a wild bird trapped in there. He's flying around, but that spotted dog isn't even bothered by him. In fact, they're acting like they're friends or something. I've never seen anything like it!"

Mr. Cooper explained the situation, and everyone seemed to enjoy the sight, but Martha was not quite happy. She knew that if Chipper was able to get out of his cage and fly around the trailer, then soon he would be able to take care of himself. Soon she would need to set him free, but she wasn't ready for that yet. She told herself that Chipper still needed her for food, and he really liked his evening perch on the warm light. Mom agreed with her that it wasn't time to release Chipper yet.

As she closed her eyes that night, Martha prayed, "God, let me do what's right for Chipper. I'd like to keep him a long time. But if he needs to be free someday, please be sure he has plenty of food and everything he needs. Amen."

The day before the Coopers headed for home, they found a field where they could pick their own wild Maine blueberries. The berries were big and juicy and delicious. They picked a lot, ate most of them before they got back to the trailer, but saved a few to eat during the drive home.

Martha and Dad heard Mrs. Cooper laughing while she was washing the blueberries. They went inside the trailer to see what was so funny. Chipper had discovered the sweetness of the blueberries and wanted more than Mom would give him. He decided to get some for himself. With a quick little hop, Chipper landed on the end of the sink faucet. Before Mom could stop him, he reached down and snatched a berry. Then he slid down the back of the faucet just like a kid at a playground. After he ate the blueberry he would do it all over again for another berry. Chipper always grabbed the biggest berries too. Chipper seemed particularly fat and content when he perched on his lampshade that night.

Late in the afternoon of the first day back on the road the family drove past a campground. "Not yet," thought Mr. Cooper, "We can *still* drive for awhile and find another spot to camp farther south."

They drove and drove and drove. It was going to be dark soon, but there were no campgrounds in sight. There wasn't much of anything in sight, except for cornfields and woods. Finally, the tired travelers found a gas station and pulled over. Mr. Cooper asked the manager if they could park the trailer there and spend the night.

Martha carried Chipper's cage into the trailer, and Mom started getting dinner ready. Mr. Cooper took Pride for a walk. By now, the sun was down, and the manager had turned on the bright gas station lights. As Mr. Cooper opened the door to let Pride in the trailer, Chipper darted out the door and flew toward the lights outside the trailer.

Martha jumped up and ran after the bird. He had to be close by! He wouldn't just fly away. There he was! He was headed toward the tall trees in the woods behind the gas station. Dad and Mom headed after Martha, who was headed after the bird.

Martha couldn't understand why Chipper was ignoring her calls to him. He kept flying higher and deeper into the woods. Tears ran down Martha's face as she realized that Chipper wasn't going to come to her. Now it was getting so dark she couldn't see him at all. She sobbed as she headed back to the trailer. Mr. Cooper felt awful and said he would keep looking for awhile. Angry and hurt, Martha said she didn't care about that old bird anyway. But when she reached the trailer, she threw herself into her mother's arms and sobbed, "I want Chipper."

Mom had tears in her eyes as she tried to comfort her daughter. The whole family had come to love that little bird, and nobody was ready to see him go. They ate a quiet dinner, and even Pride seemed sad. Before she went to bed that night, Martha called outside for Chipper one last time. No answer. She got ready for bed and hugged Pride close to her as she cried herself to sleep.

The next morning, the family tried to cheer each other up. Mr. Cooper felt like it was his fault for opening the door. But he chuckled when Mom joked, "How else were you supposed to get in? Slide under the crack?"

"Mom, Chipper is supposed to be free. We said that from the beginning. We were just going to take care of him until he could take care of himself. Well, now he can take care of himself. He's ready to be on his own. After all, we still have Pride. She needs us to take care of her," Martha said.

Pride barked. It seemed like she was agreeing with Martha, but Dad said it was time for Pride's walk. He got her leash and, as the two headed out the door, both Martha and Mom decided to go with them. They looked and listened for Chipper, but they never found him. What they did find was enough to show them just how wonderfully God had answered Martha's prayers.

Chipper's new home was surrounded by corn fields and wheat fields. Yellow sunflowers grew in a field of their own. Chipper would have plenty of food, and there was a small creek for water and his baths. He could make his home in the tall treetops in the woods, and Martha saw wild blueberry bushes. Many birds flew around them, so Martha was sure Chipper would find some friends. Best of all was the gas station. If Chipper got lonely for a warm night-light before he fell asleep, he could always head over to the gas station lights and find some warmth there.

As the family drove back onto the highway, Martha took one last look behind her. Thanks God, she thought. Thank You for giving Chipper to us for awhile. We'll never know if he is a boy cardinal or a girl cardinal, but we do know that, thanks to You and us, Chipper is a happy cardinal.

Martha gave Pride a hug and smiled as her

family headed back to Maryland.

PINE CONE TREATS

Materials
- Cotton string or twine
- Pine cones
- $\frac{1}{4}$ cup chunky peanut butter
- A pie pan filled with any of the following:
    commercial birdseed mix
    sunflower seeds
    cereals
    raisins
    shelled peanut pieces
    walnut or pecan pieces
    dried bread crumbs
    halved cranberries
    coconut
    corn bread crumbs
- Table knife
- Scissors

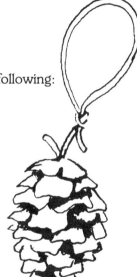

Wrap the string around the stem end of a pine cone and tie it with a knot. Loop the other end over and tie a knot as shown so that you have a loop of string attached to the pine cone. Spread peanut butter on the cone. Roll cone in the birdseed and treats in the pie pan. Hang the pine cone outside in the open, where birds will be able to see approaching predators.

Lily's Pond

On a Sunday afternoon, just after her fourth birthday, Lily came running to her mother in tears. She had been merrily chasing her brothers when she accidentally stepped into one of the many soft spots in the yard. Her pretty church shoes stayed in the mud, and her white ruffled socks were now green with stains and wet.

Mother hugged the sobbing child and looked at her husband. "It's time," she said.

Her husband nodded his head and said the backhoe would be here next Saturday to work on the new driveway. They could do it then.

Looking back, Lily remembered the day the backhoe came. The whole family was fascinated with the way the incredibly noisy machine gracefully moved loads of grass and dirt. With one smooth motion the driver reached for a targeted spot, bit into the soil with the shovel, and then swung it over to waiting pickup trucks.

For years, Mr. McKay had been planning to put in a pond. Their old house was set on a hill, and the huge front yard was full of underground springs. That's why the lawn was so squishy in places. Adding the pond and cutting in the stream to the bottom of the hill would drain those springs away from the children's play area.

The family worked on the project together. The first winter they let the small pond settle. By the next spring the pond was almost three feet deep in the deepest part, and at least six inches or deeper everywhere else. The overflow pipe that Mr. McKay installed directed the water from the spring-fed pond to the little stream that ran down the hill.

It was time to start thinking about the ecosystem that would naturally develop in the water and along its banks. The McKays bought some oxygenating plants to keep the algae population under control. By the following year these small floating plants were well-established and kept the water clear.

Frogs and toads had moved in to lay their eggs in the pond. Every spring the water was full of clumps of frog eggs and strings of toad eggs. Lily and her brother watched the development of the tadpoles as they grew legs and reabsorbed their tails. Mrs. McKay took Lily to a fish hatchery, and they picked out some young carp to add to their pond. Mother helped Lily plant beautiful flowers by the pond and along the banks of the stream.

For the next two years the entire family enjoyed the pond life. The children could count as many as 40 fish. In the heat of the afternoon, as many as a dozen frogs would be sitting on rocks or just poking their bulging eyes out of the water. Waders could always uncover a crayfish, and even an occasional salamander.

The kids tried to gently catch any creature they saw. The only rule was that no animal could be removed from the pond to keep in a tank or aquarium. It was strictly a catch-marvel-and-release operation. Unfortunately, the heron that came to visit didn't know the rules.

Lily was 10 years old when she and Mother first saw the big bluish-gray bird. Looking down from the front porch, it looked like a blue log resting on the water. Mrs. McKay was wondering who threw that in when Lily realized it was a bird. They got the bird book and discovered it was a blue heron.

As they left the house and headed to the store, Lily and Mother discussed the ecosystem that had evolved because of Lily's pond. Her parents had explained long ago that, as wilderness areas are developed for human use, it's important to see that protected areas are left for God's other creatures. Lily's little pond, that wasn't any bigger than the floor in her room, had become a home for thousands of God's creatures, from darting dragon files to the long-legged heron.

When they returned from the store, Lily and Mother knew something was wrong as soon as they pulled into their driveway. Mr. McKay and the boys stood quietly by the pond. Dad was shaking his head from side to side, and the boys were searching the surface.

The big bird they had so admired in the morning had gobbled up practically every sign of life in the small pond. Without large plants or logs to hide under, the fish and frogs, and maybe even the crayfish, had become easy prey for the hungry bird.

"Well, we can chase the bird away when we see it," Dad said, "but that doesn't seem like the most natural way to protect the few fish and frogs we have left."

"No, it doesn't," Mother agreed. "And after all, the bird was only trying to feed itself and maybe its family. We need to provide some big water plants, and maybe even a submerged log, so at least the little creatures have a chance of protecting themselves from the bird." That's when the real gardening began.

Lily's brothers were all in high school or

beyond now. They didn't have time for the frog hunting and wading adventures that the pond offered, so Lily and Mother started planning their water garden. They planted cattails and irises in the bog areas below the pond. Directly in the pond they added potted water lilies and smaller water plants. The first summer, the plants grew to provide wonderful coverage for the year's new population of frogs and fish.

The following spring Lily's friend, Alicia, turned 11. Alicia invited girls and boys to her birthday party. Lily thought that nobody really had a good time. The boys were bored, so they teased the girls. The girls hated the teasing and ran from the boys. The boys got in trouble for chasing the girls. The girls got in trouble for messing up their party clothes. All in all, it was pretty much a disaster. As Lily and Mother discussed the party, they thought there must be a way for both boys and girls to have fun at the same party.

Lily and her mother took on the challenge and picked a summer date for Lily's party. It would be a year's end party for her friends at school. It would be a garden party. A garden party with a twist.

Lily started planning the party and designing the invitations. Classmates were always teasing her about her name. Once when a teacher held up a paper tablet that had been left on the playground, a boy said, "Oh, that's Lily's pad," and some other boys started croaking like frogs. Sometimes they called her Easter Lily. It used to bother Lily. But then a girl named Rose joined the class. The boys touched her arm and ran away screaming about pricking their finger on a rose thorn. Rose and Lily became good friends and learned to ignore the teasing.

For this party, Lily was going to use her name to make her party even more interesting. The McKay family laughed when they saw the invitation Lily had made. Lily wanted to invite the whole class and the teacher. That would be 18 guests.

A few days later in the mail each guest received an invitation which read,

You're invited to Lily's pad.
Don't bring your mom, don't bring your dad,

Just bring yourself, dressed in your best,
And you'll enjoy it along with the rest.

We'll have punch and cookies and cake that is sweet,
And enjoy flowers from my garden which can't be beat,

And for you who are interested in Lily's pond,
You'll see frogs and lizards in tanks on the ground.

So celebrate the best school year we've had,
With all the creatures at Lily's pad.

Mrs. McKay cleaned up an old aquarium. Later she found her grandmother's punch bowl and washed all the crystal punch cups. Dad volunteered to barbecue hamburgers and hot dogs. Mother and Lily baked dozens of cookies ahead of time and planned to have carrot sticks, potato chips, and a decorated cake for the occasion.

Lily's brothers set out some Frisbees to play with (away from the food tables) and set up the croquet set.

Mr. McKay borrowed tables from church. Lily already knew what she was going to wear for the party. Her finest dress was safely hanging in the closet, and her Sunday shoes were ready and waiting. Now came the fun part.

In their absolute grubbiest work clothes, Mother and daughter cleaned out the weeds and rotting leaves from the narrow stream bed. For this party, the yard had to look its best. As they cleaned, they uncovered one huge salamander and two smaller ones. These creatures would spend the night in the aquarium. Lily hurried to add all the comforts the amphibians would appreciate. She put on her swimsuit and some tall boots and ever so carefully waded into the pond. She cleaned away the spent blossoms of her precious water lilies and managed to grab a big, lazy frog before she climbed out of the water.

Mother and Lily caught two more frogs from the side of the pond. The frogs went into a bucket with a screen lid and would be special guests at the party as well. Lily had been only knee-deep in the pond, but with all the flower trimming and frog-catching activity, she was dirty from head to toe. With her hair falling in her eyes and mud streaks across her cheeks, her mother ran to get the camera. This mud duck was hardly recognizable as the same young lady who would host a garden party the following day.

From the time the guests arrived until the party was over, everyone had a great time. The cookies were fancy, the food was delicious, and everybody enjoyed studying the invited creatures from Lily's pond. The highlight of the day was the frog jumping contest. Lily picked three kids from the class to carry the frogs to the starting line. They stepped back and everybody cheered as the frogs hopped back to the pond. First one to splash was the winner. The boys couldn't believe that Lily had caught the frogs herself the day before.

Too soon it was time for her guests to go home. To signal the end of the celebration, Lily asked Mrs. Grayson, her teacher, to have the honor of releasing the salamanders, crayfish, and tadpoles that had been so interesting to study up close during the day.

After the last guest had left and Lily's family was cleaning up, Mother couldn't help but think back to the four-year-old girl who had cried when she ruined her shoes while chasing the boys. She's really grown, Mrs. McKay thought. She's learned to be a gracious hostess, and she's learned to care for God's beautiful world, thanks to God's creatures and this wonderful pond.

THE WORLD'S SMALLEST WATER GARDEN

Materials

- Two tablespoons of alfalfa seeds (available from health food stores)
- Quart jar with a canning-lid ring
- Cheesecloth or clean nylon mesh
- Water

Place two tablespoons of seeds in the jar. Cover them with water, cover the jar with cheesecloth or mesh, and let the seeds soak overnight.

Keep the jar in a dark place. Rinse and drain the seeds well three times a day, for about a week. After a couple of days, you will notice little white sprouts growing from the seeds.

After four days move the jar onto a window sill, but don't let the sprouts dry out or get too hot. When the jar is full of green sprouts you can start lifting out forkfuls to put on your sandwiches or to toss with a salad. They are wonderful in pita-bread sandwiches!

Store remaining sprouts in the refrigerator in a covered container. Discard any limp, soggy sprouts. These are no longer fresh.

My Nightmare

Dad reminded me to take out the trash before I went to bed. I forgot.

When I was in bed, Mom asked me if I had taken out the trash. I pretended to be asleep. Pretty soon, I was.

The dream started out innocently enough. I was cheerfully carrying out the trash to the cans behind the garage. I knew right away it was a dream, because I'm never cheerful when I take out the garbage. As I dragged the bag around the corner of the garage, I stopped dead in my tracks. The cans were already full. They were overflowing. There was trash everywhere. When I looked closer, one can had eyes and had come to life. It didn't move around; it just sat still and munched on something. "Chomp, chomp, chomp," over and over. Finally, it burped and grunted, "Feed me."

I was frightened, but again it demanded, "Feed me!" I looked at the trash bag in my hands, then carefully walked nearer to the talking can. When I held the trash bag near enough to the huge mouth, the can snatched at the bag and started its rhythmic chewing. Suddenly, the can spit out most of the contents of the bag. Soft drink cans ricocheted off the garage wall. Newspapers went flying through the air, and an empty paper-towel roll went whizzing by my left ear.

"More!" the can called. I searched the area for anything that would quiet the can. After a lot of trial and error, I realized it would eat all the food scraps from the kitchen, and even the pruned pieces from Mom's houseplants. At last the can seemed satisfied, and that was good, because I couldn't find a single banana peel or lettuce leaf anywhere to feed it.

But there was still a mountain of trash next to my garage. Then I heard a screeching noise as an old beat-up pickup truck drove into our alley. It screeched to a halt right next to our garage and blinked its headlights. It honked its horn, and cried "Gimme." I tried to ignore it, but it just beeped louder, "Gimme. Gimme. Gimme!"

I picked up a soft drink can and hurled it at the truck. To my surprise the truck lifted its hood and snatched the can out of mid-air. Its lights flashed and the motor said, "Mmm-mmm." It was quiet only for a moment and then started again, "Gimme, gimme, gimme!"

I reached for another piece of trash. As quickly as I hurled the old notebook at the truck, it spit it back out at me. Before long I realized that this machine only wanted cans, bottles, jars, and old newspapers. It took a while to satisfy it, but eventually I had sorted all the trash next to our garage. The truck had eaten every tuna can, soda-pop can, mayonnaise jar, milk jug, and egg carton we had.

After a while I noticed that the mountain of

trash that had first greeted me when I had come out of the house was getting smaller and smaller. The only thing left in our alley was a mountain of my kid sister's disposable diapers (good thing I can't smell in my sleep!), three detergent boxes, about a hundred little pudding containers, a bunch of single-serving drink boxes, two gallons of paint, a couple old tubes of model airplane glue, six dead batteries, an almost-empty can of drain cleaner, a pile of plastic bags of every size imaginable, and a handful of my dad's disposable razors. That was nothing compared to what was there when I started. Really!

Then I thought I heard a whisper. After a moment I heard it again. A quiet voice whispered, "Toxic."

Soon other small voices joined in with the same word. They kept whispering it over and over again, and more and more voices were adding to the chorus. Soon I realized that the two gallons of paint were leading the chorus. I ran and got a big cardboard box from the garage. Maybe the box would quiet the voices.

I put the paint cans in the box. They were quiet! It worked. As I placed the empty can of drain cleaner in the box, it stopped talking. The same with the tubes of model glue.

The last voices I had trouble tracking. They were the tiny voices that kept singing "Toxic." Finally I realized it was the innocent-looking dead batteries. All six of them went into the cardboard box. I drew a skull and crossbones on the box and placed it high on a shelf outside the garage. I would figure out what to do with that in a moment.

I bagged up everything that remained and hurried to catch up with a trash truck I'd spied driving around the corner. The driver saw me waving frantically and stopped. When he saw my bags of trash, he shook his head and said, "No way. Not any more. There's no more room for your trash. You'll just have to keep it."

I stood there with my mouth open as the truck pulled away. Just then, still in my dream, I heard my mother calling, "Derek, it's time for spring cleaning! Let's get this basement cleaned out. Next we'll tackle the attic. Derek, it's time for spring cleaning!"

"Oh, no!" I cried, "Where will all this stuff go?" I was left holding the bag, and I woke up from the dream in a sweat.

"Derek," my mom called, "Let's get started with spring cleaning."

I realized she was calling for real. This wasn't a dream any longer, but the meaning of the dream was clear to me.

"Hey Dad," I said at the breakfast table, "how about that compost pile you wanted to start behind the garage? Can I help you get that started this morning?"

Dad was caught off guard by my eagerness to help. "Why, sure you can." He stood up from the table before he had even finished his breakfast. "Let's go," he said.

As he gathered the materials needed to construct his bin, I searched the garage for large empty boxes. I found two. I knew I would need more containers, good, strong containers, so I headed for the trash cans behind the garage. I held my breath as I turned the corner, recalling the snarling, gruesome characters from my dream. All I saw were our innocent, recently emptied cans. What a relief. I grabbed them both and dragged them to the backyard.

I took a piece of chalk and wrote on the sidewalk next to one can, *Toxic Waste*, and next to the second can I wrote *Landfill*. I had special labels for the boxes too. I wrote *To Be Recycled* across the flap of the first one, and on the second I wrote *Reusable*.

By the time Mom got back from dropping my baby sister off at Grandma's, Dad and I had the compost bin set up. It was ready to receive all grass clippings, raked leaves, and vegetable scraps.

We headed back to the house, and Dad and I became the runners as Mom barked the orders. She had sorted through dressers and removed all the clothes we had outgrown or just didn't wear. "Reusable," she said, and dad carried the clothes down to the box in the garage. She told me to go through my old toy box. I found toys to give away, toys to recycle, and a bunch of dead batteries that had to go in the can marked, *Toxic*. I would have to put rechargeable batteries on my Christmas list. We went through the baby's room in the same way.

We moved through every room of the house, searching, sorting, and stacking all through the morning. Just before lunch we tackled the basement. When we were through down there, we had added five quarts of used motor oil to the toxic can, and bunches of stuff, including repairable furniture, to the reusable pile. After finishing the basement we were more than ready for lunch. Mom made sandwiches and reached for some paper plates.

"That's okay," I said, "we'll just eat them outside on the grass." Before she could grab the juice boxes from the refrigerator, I found a big can of grape juice in the pantry. "This looks good," I said. We poured the juice into a pitcher and carried our sandwiches outside. The juice can was destined for the box marked *To Be Recycled.* I pitched the crust from my sandwiches into the compost bin, and drank my juice out of a real glass.

Well, you get the idea. The afternoon went

much like the morning. By quitting time we had sorted through every room in the house and the garage as well.

Mom made a phone call to arrange a pick-up time for the donation of all our reusable items. Dad loaded up the car with all the recyclables and took them to the recycling center. He picked up my baby sister on the way home. The toxic materials were stored high up on a garage shelf until we could find out when the next Household Hazardous Waste Collection Day would be. I had the pleasure of taking out the garbage. I practically skipped to the cans behind the garage, cheerfully carrying a very manageable bag in one hand. I emptied the bag into the can. Out tumbled a tired old pair of slippers, an old set of yellow pages, and a broken pair of glasses.

I heard Dad calling to me, "Derek, let's go have a snack."

I threw one more look back at the trash can and smiled. I don't think I'll be having nightmares tonight!

A SHOPPING SPREE

Plan a trip to the grocery store with your family or class. Discuss the following questions.

- Are vegetables and fruits available in loose form, or are they prepackaged on foam trays wrapped with plastic?
- Are the trays in the meat department made of foam or fiberboard?
- For school lunches, which is the better packaging choice: Two three-packs of 10-ounce juice boxes for $1.50 each, or a recyclable 64-ounce can priced at $1.30? How could you carry your juice to school if it didn't come in individual-size containers?
- Which choice shows better stewardship of our natural resources: Paper grocery bags, plastic grocery bags, or reusable shopping bags? Why?
- How can you avoid using zillions of little plastic bags in your school lunch every year?
- In what ways do some products try to trick you into thinking that they are best for the environment?
- If you could change anything about the way people in our country buy groceries, what would you change?
- Discuss what is meant by the phrase *Convenience for today may mean inconvenience tomorrow.*

Scooter's Scouts

The screen door slammed shut at the same time that Tracey sobbed, "Mom!"

Twelve-year-old Scooter jumped up from his reading and started toward his little sister.

"Mom's at the store, Tracey. What happened?"

Tracey had been riding her bike home from her friend's house when Jeff and Dale caught up to her on their bikes and started teasing her. Tracey said they were trying to crowd her off the road, but she just kept pedaling.

Scooter knew the two boys from school. He knew Jeff and Dale wouldn't hurt Tracey, but she didn't know that.

That evening, Scooter convinced Tracey to tell her parents what had happened. Dad asked Tracey if she would be able to forgive them. Tracey thought for a moment. She'd be able to forgive them, but she didn't think those boys would care if they were forgiven.

Scooter thought one of the problems was the design of their new neighborhood. The developers had remembered to put hiking trails in the community, but bikes weren't allowed on those, and bikers couldn't get to the big lake trail without loading their bikes onto bike racks and driving them over. Maybe Jeff and Dale were bored on school-day afternoons with so little space to ride their bikes.

Scooter's dad agreed with him, and together the family came up with an idea to improve the situation. Mr. McIntosh got out a map of the development to see if their idea would work. On paper it looked like it would.

The homeowners' association was having a meeting next week. That would be enough time for Scooter to prepare a good presentation and get a couple supporters to agree to help with his idea.

Mr. McIntosh and Scooter drew his proposed bike path on the map next to the existing hiking trail. It would work perfectly to connect the neighborhood with the wide lakeside path that already allowed bikes without disturbing the hikers on the footpath.

Scooter already knew that the adults in the association didn't like the idea of a bike path because they were sure the teenagers would vandalize it or leave trash behind. So the whole family came up with ideas that would encourage the neighborhood children and teens to respect the trail.

The very next day Scooter saw Dale and Jeff hanging out on the corner down the street. He took a deep breath and walked over to them. "Hi, guys. My dad and I worked out a plan for building a new bike path. I could use your help at the homeowners meeting."

Jeff and Dale looked at each other, nodded their heads, and agreed to help. "Hey, Scooter," Dale said. He seemed embarrassed. "I thought you were coming over to give us grief about bothering Tracey yesterday."

"Oh, yeah." said Scooter, "About that. She would like you to apologize."

The boys agreed to meet one time before they made their presentation. Jeff and Dale brought three friends with them and had good news too. Dale's mom worked for the park service. She would be able to have some signs made for their bike trail, small signs that would mark special points of interest such as the spot where the bike path would cross the birdwatchers' bluebird trail, as well as a larger sign that listed the rules of the trail.

Scooter laughed. "The adults will be glad to hear that."

Jeff's stepfather wanted to help with the project as well. He saw that the boys were planning not only a trail with two banked turns and a ramp area, but were also going to have a wildflower meadow and an overlook. He offered to buy the seeds and provide trees from his landscaping business. That way the trail would be beautiful as well as inviting to animals like rabbits and songbirds.

The evening of the presentation, nine young people came to the meeting with their parents to show support for the proposed bike path. Scooter was nervous, but he did a good job describing the bike path he and the others had designed. He told the adults about the ramp and banked turns. He also reminded them that all riders promised to wear the required safety gear. Tracey held up the posters she and her mother had made. The posters showed the landscaping contributions Jeff's stepfather would make. The crowd was impressed. One woman thought Scooter should tell the newspaper about the plans to attract birds and wildlife.

The presentation was going well until one burly man stood up and asked in a deep voice how the children would enforce the rules. "How are you going to make sure riders follow the rules and don't start causing trouble?" he boomed.

Jeff and Dale stood up tall and stepped up to the microphone. They looked directly at the big man and said, "We will."

That was all they said, but they stayed standing without taking their eyes off the man who asked the question. He sat down, satisfied that the boys would be able to handle the job.

Scooter smiled. He and his family were delighted to have the support of all the bike riders in the area. The vote was unanimous. Everyone thought the bike path was a good idea. After the meeting was over, Jeff and Dale came over to Tracey. "You did a good job on the posters, Tracey," said Jeff, "They really helped to win our case."

"Yeah," Dale agreed. Then he added, "And we're sorry about the other day. We should have left you alone."

Tracey stood wide-eyed and surprised. "Thank you," she managed to say.

The kids and parents started working the next weekend under the direction of Scooter, Jeff, and Jeff's stepfather. The future looked good for the residents of the neighborhood, the bike riders, hikers, and wildlife as well.

BE A LAND DEVELOPER

Think about the area where you live. Do you think another park or hiking path would be a nice addition? Many towns have turned abandoned railroad tracks into nature trails for hikers, bikers, and even horseback riders. Is there public space available for such a project? How could you find out?

If your house is in a development, there is usually a homeowners association. Someone there can answer your questions. If you live in a town or city, call your city hall. In rural areas, check with your county zoning office. It's important to have the support and involvement of your parents or school for a project like this.

If you like to design parks, houses, or entire communities, you might want to be an architect, a landscape designer, or even a developer. God has provided land for people to use; it is one of our natural resources. It's up to us to use it wisely. Spaces must be provided for people to live and to play. Don't forget spaces for God's wild creatures and their needs. *Always* include plenty of trees.

Cat Smiles

It isn't easy being the youngest, but days like today make it all worth it, Laura thought. She knew that if she didn't have an older sister and brother to go with her, she never would be able to go ice skating on the frozen creek. Laura turned to say good-bye to the smiling metal cat as they headed home. It wasn't so long ago that its face didn't seem like it was smiling, and it was all because of Laura's older brother and sister that the expression had changed.

Cathy was 10 last spring, and Dennis turned 13. They loved going to the park, even when it meant taking Laura along. The park followed the creek in both directions through town.

The creek fascinated the children. Often they lifted rocks, looking for crayfish. Sometimes they had picnics on the large rock island in the creek. And once they had tried to dam the creek by piling stones between the island and the bank.

The big cat was just upstream of the rock island. It wasn't a real cat. It was a big, rust-colored, round iron plate set in concrete. Two metal hinges at the top looked like ears, and someone had painted the eyes and face on the cat. The cat face was taller than Laura, but not as tall as Cathy or Dennis. Dennis said it covered up the outlet of the town's storm sewer. There was another one just like it that the children passed on their walk to school.

Laura understood what the storm sewer was. There was an opening to it at the bottom of the hill next to their house. When it rained, the water ran down the hill and then drained into the opening of the sewer. The water would continue to flow in a big sewer pipe until it came to the cat face at the creek. There it would slowly seep into the creek water and continue on its way.

Dennis said it was because of this sewer water that they couldn't take off their shoes and wade in the creek. One time, Dennis' friend, Tommy, went wading. Laura wanted to try it too. Her brother and sister wouldn't let her, and on their next walk home from school they showed her why. Where the water from the second cat face came into the creek, oily grease floated on top of the water. Brown and yellow sudsy bubbles floated on top of the water, too, and the water smelled awful. The oily patches reflected pretty colors of blue, green, and purple, just like bubbles you blow with a bubble wand, but Dennis said the water was polluted. Laura wasn't exactly sure what that meant, but Cathy explained to her that no crayfish or anything could live in this water because it wasn't clean enough. It was too dirty with yuck from the storm sewer.

Laura thought the bubbles must come from everybody's washing machines. She thought they were brown and yellow because they had carried away the dirt from the clothes. She felt

bad, and it wasn't until Dennis and Cathy used the cat faces and creek for a science report that they learned the real cause of the polluted water.

Cathy and Dennis collected four water samples. Two from where the water came out of each cat face, and two in deep water areas of the creek. One creek water sample came from far upstream, so it didn't have any storm sewer water in it. Another sample of creek water was taken from right around the island where Tommy had gone wading.

Mom and Dad helped Cathy and Dennis pay a laboratory to have the water samples tested. The water sample from way upstream was the cleanest. The storm-sewer water from the cat closest to the children's house contained garden fertilizer and some motor oil, but not nearly as much motor oil as the water from the cat face closer to school. That water contained not only motor oil, but gasoline as well. There were also high amounts of phosphates and detergents. The creek water where Tommy had waded showed the same results, but it was more diluted. Now Dennis and Cathy had to determine the sources for all these pollutants.

Cathy got a street map that showed their neighborhood, but that wasn't much help. Dennis said they would use it to make a topographical map. They would draw in the hills in the area, and then they could find where the water was coming from that went into the storm sewer. Dennis carried Cathy's road map with him, and they marked the hills on the map as they walked to school.

After school that day the kids waited for Mom to meet them with the car. They weren't looking forward to going to the dentist, but they would be able to mark more hills on their street map.

The school was at the top of a hill next to a busy street. On the same street there were many offices, a gas station and car wash, a flower shop, and a pet store. There was also a storm sewer opening. As Mom drove along the street, Dennis and Kathy watched a gas station worker hosing down the area with a water hose. The water, of course, ran toward the storm sewer. It would take one more water sample to be sure, but Cathy and Dennis were sure the oil, gasoline, and detergents were coming from this gas station and car wash. Later that same evening, Cathy and Dennis rode back with their dad and collected a water sample from a puddle near the gas station's storm sewer.

When the test results came back from the lab, Dennis and Cathy finished up their report. They got an *A*, and the science teacher asked them what they would do next. Dennis and Cathy hadn't thought about that.

At dinner that night the family discussed their next step. Dad would go with Dennis and Cathy to talk to the owner of the car wash. They were sure that the phosphates and detergents were coming from his business. They would also make a flyer to take to all the homes in the neighborhood, telling them about the fertilizer in the creek water. It must have been coming from the green lawns nearby. Dad suggested that the kids learn about alternative products that were better for the creek before they talked to all these people. So they did.

Since the owner of the car wash lived in the same neighborhood, he, too, was concerned about the water in the creek. He didn't know his business was causing a problem. When he read the report and saw the test results, he agreed to change to a soap that would be less harmful. He also used an absorbent material to clean up the spilled gasoline and oil. Since he already collected used motor oil for recycling, it was easy to send away the oil-soaked litter as well.

Cathy and Dennis were never sure whether any neighbors started using a safer lawn fertilizer, but they liked to think they helped to make a difference. They planned to take more water samples after a few more months, but Laura was certain the water was cleaner already. She said the cats looked happier these days.

BE A WATER CYCLE DETECTIVE

Under our towns, cities, and housing developments, a special water pipe system carries water to our homes from urban water supplies and carries waste water away from our homes. The waste water includes all the water from our sinks, dishwashers, bathtubs, toilets, and wash machines.

Waste water used to be dumped into the ocean, but that's illegal now. Some communities compost their waste water and turn it into fertilizer. Others burn the solid waste, dump it in a landfill, or use it on farmland and other undeveloped land. Which do you think is best for God's green earth?

• What happens to waste water in your community? Call your city water department or your state's environmental department.

• Design a water cycle that shows where your tap water comes from and how it gets to your house. Then show where it goes after it leaves your home as waste water. Try to find out how it is treated and processed. Where does it finally end up? In order for a process to be a true cycle, the end product has to work its way back to the beginning stage and return to its original form.

• If you live in a rural area and use well water and a septic system, your water also has a cycle. The water should be purified through natural microbial action and plenty of filtering before it returns to the ground water aquifers that keep your well full. You can draw a path that shows your complete water cycle as well.

Hooray for the Honkers

M̲r. Barklage organized the overnight trip for the fifth- and sixth-grade students who attended Calvary Church. Mr. Barklage wanted to set up a junior youth group.

Five boys and three girls had signed up for the hiking trip. Certainly enough kids to organize a junior youth group. A hike up Old Rag Mountain wasn't the toughest hike around, but it was going to be a challenge.

"We're almost there," said Mr. Barklage, checking his map. Sure enough, after they pulled off the interstate, they could see the range in the distance. When Mr. Barklage stopped at a gas station to refuel, everybody was ready for a rest stop. Mr. Barklage stepped out of the van and felt like he walked into a wall of hot air. The kids groaned about the heat, especially after riding in the comfort of the air-conditioned van.

When they finally arrived at the drop-off point, Mike suggested they just drive the van all the way to the top. Mr. Barklage thought that wasn't such a bad idea, but there was no road to the top! The only way to get to the peak of Old Rag was by foot.

They locked up the van and started out. Mr. Barklage led the procession. Every hiker carried a backpack with food, sleeping bag, Bible, flashlight, and clothes. A couple boys had pup-tent bundles tied to their packs, and Mr. Barklage had the first-aid kit and a few other supplies with him.

The hikers walked along a nicely wooded path, gently sloping up toward the mountain. A stream babbled happily beside the hikers' path. But this was just the beginning.

The line of hikers snaking up the path had broken up into segments, some here, some there, after an hour of hiking. Mr. Barklage stayed in front to keep the more energetic from getting too far ahead of the others. The heat was beginning to take its toll. Several hikers slowed down.

"Mr. Barklage!" Suddenly all the kids were yelling at once. He hurried back to find the hikers huddled around Tanya. She had fallen to the ground. Seth and Mike were trying to pull off her backpack. Beth had taken a bandanna down to the creek to get some cool water. Tanya lay without moving, her eyes closed. Everybody shouted orders at once.

"Elevate her feet!"

"Lift up her head!"

"Cool her off!"

"Cover her up!"

Mr. Barklage stepped in. He saw the flushed look, felt the dry skin, and realized Tanya was overheated. He took the bandanna from Beth and gently placed it behind Tanya's neck. She blinked her eyes, and her hands reached toward the cool cloth. Mr. Barklage called for the boys to get more cool cloths. They placed those

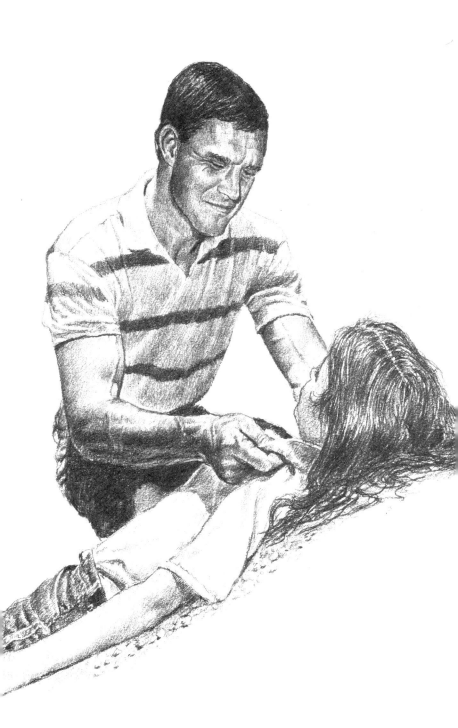

on Tanya's wrists and under her knees. Everybody offered to share their own drinking water when Mr. Barklage asked the group for a drink for the rapidly recovering girl. Tanya sat up—a bit shaken, but definitely okay.

When everyone's pulse returned to normal, Mr. Barklage suggested that one of the first group activities of this new junior youth group could be a first-aid class. They could even invite the senior high kids to attend. "Or we could not invite them," he smiled when he saw the disapproving looks on the faces of his hikers.

They were only about an hour from the ridge when the trail changed from a pleasant wooded path to a narrow climb between rock walls. This would be the toughest part of the climb. Mr. Barklage gave up his lead position to stay farther back and help stragglers lift their packs up to ledges before they hoisted themselves up.

The kids loved it. The air was cooler. And the hikers could rest as they climbed from here to there, one at a time. Seth and Brandon were in front now, and they, along with Beth, scoped out the trail ahead of them and picked the best path to take through the rocky crags and crevices.

No longer looking like a line of ducks, the hiking group more resembled a family of mountain goats scampering on a mountainside. When Mr. Barklage pointed out this resemblance, Tanya suggested their group be called the Calvary Kids.

As the ascent continued through the rougher area, Lin began falling behind. He didn't realize how close he was to the top when he just plain gave up. He couldn't go any farther with his pack on his back. It was time for the whole group to take a break anyway, before their final surge to the top of Old Rag.

The group sat on the rock ledges and looked out over the valley. The air was clear where they were, but they looked down on a reddish-brown layer of smog. It wasn't a very pleasant sight, and Lin wondered if this ugly view was how the mountain got its ugly name, Old Rag.

"I don't think so," Mr. Barklage said. "This mountain has been called Old Rag since before

Abraham Lincoln was president. Just wait 'til you see the view from the top," he added. "You'll be able to see the other side of the mountain, where there isn't as much smog."

Ready to move on, Seth and Brandon decided to stay back with Lin. He felt he could keep going if he didn't have to carry his own pack. Lin was packing an old canvas knapsack, with no frame to help distribute the load.

When Seth lifted the old pack over his shoulder, he was almost knocked off balance by the weight of the extra load. He was amazed at the difference a backpack frame could make. He quickly learned to fling the extra pack ahead of him before he tried any climbs. Soon Seth, too, needed to be relieved of the bulky knapsack.

Brandon took the heavy load, and soon he and Lin and Seth could hear shouts from the rest of the hikers as they reached the top. Beth raced back to encourage these last three.

"The view is really worth the trip," she assured them. "And besides, it will be time for supper when you get to the top." The three boys could see that Mr. Barklage had started a campfire, and they knew the peak was just a short climb away.

The two Good Samaritans were left holding the knapsack as the owner of the sack raced to the campfire with Beth. Seth and Brandon looked at each other dumbfounded, shook their heads, and grabbed the straps of the knapsack between them. With war whoops and hollers of "Charge!" the two stormed forward, passed Harry and Erika still on the trail, and raced into camp. They threw down the knapsack with their last bit of energy and collapsed at Mr. Barklage's feet.

"Everyone present and accounted for," gasped Brandon as he lifted his head and then let it drop again.

Mr. Barklage laughed, not at Brandon on the ground, but at the contents of the old knapsack, spilled out on the ground. It wasn't the design of the knapsack that made it so heavy. It was the dozen or more cans of soda, baked beans, ravioli, pudding, and fruit cocktail that had been in the sack! Lin couldn't believe his eyes.

"What was my mother thinking!" he exclaimed. "Next time, I do my own packing!"

"Well, I hope she packed a can opener," Mr. Barklage laughed.

As the sun began to set, the Calvary Kids gathered around the campfire for supper. No supper ever tasted better than the meal those campers enjoyed that evening. Mr. Barklage listened as the kids made suggestions for the youth group. It would have to be fun. A place to talk about things that might be happening at school. Or at home.

"I'd like to see us make a difference," Erika suggested. "Like the first-aid class, but even more."

"Maybe we could work together on a project," said Harry. "Maybe do something together that we wouldn't be able to do by ourselves."

Beth remembered two kids who couldn't come on the hike because of allergies and asthma. "Could we fight against air pollution?" she asked.

The kids were on a roll now. Mr. Barklage smiled. They had climbed Old Rag. Now they thought they could conquer the world. But God wanted His people to take care of His world, and cleaning up the air was a good way to start. As they tossed around ideas, Mr. Barklage got caught up in the plans. Maybe these kids are just persistent enough to make a difference, he thought.

"If you guys are going to tackle a major project, you have to think like a goose," Mr. Barklage started. With a statement like that, he had everyone's attention.

"When the weather starts to cool off in the fall, a goose wants to fly south to warmer areas, but he just doesn't take off by himself. No way. That would be like a small child deciding he wanted to climb Old Rag by himself. The chances are a goose flying by himself just wouldn't be able to make the long, long trip alone. But he doesn't give up on the idea. Not at all. Just like you shouldn't give up on an idea like clean air.

"Anyway, the goose starts talking to some other geese, and those geese talk to other geese, and pretty soon the whole gaggle of geese wants to fly south together."

"Just like we want to fight air pollution together," suggested Seth from beyond the campfire.

"That's right," agreed Mr. Barklage. "The geese decide to work together to fly south. If they just took off and started flying, they would become exhausted. So they decide to fly in a 'V' shape. It's the most efficient, and that's probably the shape this group should use for any clean-air project.

"You see, just like we took turns being leader of the hike today, the geese take turns being leader of the V. That's the hardest spot to fly, but every spot behind the lead spot is easier. When the goose in front flaps its wings, it provides an uplift for the goose behind it, and on and on back to the geese at the end. When the lead goose gets tired, it drops back, and another takes its place. I suggest you pick a leader for your group, and when that leader gets tired, then it can be someone else's turn."

Mr. Barklage added a couple more

thoughts, "Did you know that when a goose gets sick or hurt and has to leave the V formation, two other geese also drop out and follow the ailing bird to the ground? They stay with it until it is better or it dies. Then they rejoin another formation or catch up with the first group. That's the kind of compassion I saw today with you all. I think it's important to see it continue. If we see that someone is staying away, or is feeling left out, we go to them and help them to come back.

"And don't forget the honking. All the geese behind the lead goose encourage it on with their noisy honking. I heard lots of encouraging words today. If you're going to tackle a big project like air pollution, you'll need more encouragement than you needed to climb this old mountain. Keep that in mind. Always remember the honking of the geese. The end."

As the campers headed to their sleeping bags, one voice called out above the rest, "Instead of the Calvary Kids, maybe we should call ourselves `The Honkers!'" Everyone laughed—but they agreed.

The Honkers returned home, and they began meeting every other Sunday evening. Evening meetings always included a supper and maybe a guest speaker, topic discussion, service activity, or just a game night.

An important part of the Sunday evening gathering was the *V* time. Although their parents could hardly believe it, the kids actually researched and wrote reports to share. Seth and Lin reported that, while emissions from cars, trucks, planes, and coal-burning factories are the main causes of smog, chemical plants, dry-cleaning plants, and household cleaners can also pollute the air. That night the Honkers planned a campaign asking their church members to grow more houseplants and plant more trees to absorb carbon dioxide and release oxygen. Mike and Erika volunteered to write letters to the mayor and city council asking that the city consider a tree-planting project. Mr. Barklage suggested organizing a car pool for Sunday night meetings, so each of their parents' cars weren't adding carbon dioxides to the air.

Tanya and Beth reported on the greenhouse effect. Under the ozone layer, which protects the earth from the sun's ultraviolet rays, is a blanket of gasses that help hold the warmth of the sun. Cutting down trees that process carbon dioxide and burning fossil fuels in cars, incinerators, power plants, and factories, adds "greenhouse gases" to the air and thickens the layer of insulation. The girls suggested ideas for using less electricity at home: Use fluorescent bulbs. Turn down the thermostat and wear a sweater. Turn the lights off when you leave a room.

V time ended with a sharing of ideas on what the Honkers could do next to improve the quality of their environment. Mr. Barklage often thought about the hike up Old Rag. These kids were quite a team, whether they were hiking a mountain or cleaning up the environment.

MAKE A NATURAL AIR FRESHENER

Materials
- Fabric
- Ribbon
- Sponge shapes for printing
- Tempera paint
- Cedar chips or potpourri mix
- Fabric paint or pens for writing on bag.

Sew long narrow bags out of linen or cotton woven fabric. Leave tops open. Turn right side out.

Dip sponge shapes in tempera paint to decorate bag. Write a suitable phrase with fabric paint or pens.

Allow paint to dry thoroughly.

Fill bag two-thirds full with cedar chips or potpourri. Tie with ribbon.

Becky's Christmas

Becky sighed and rolled her eyes. It was bad enough Mom had offered to help clean up after her cousin's birthday party. Now she wanted Becky to carry both extra-large, extra-full trash bags out to the alley.

Becky started to complain as she pictured herself dragging heavy trash bags through the rain all the way back to the alley. Okay, it wasn't raining; it was just a cold, gray November day. Almost raining. Still, it would take two trips to carry the monstrous bags that sat by the back door.

Becky prepared herself to heave the first bag off the ground. She was going to be extra dramatic just to show how much she resented this job. With two hands firmly grasping the bag and her knees bent, she lifted the bag with a huge groan. But the load wasn't what she expected. She spun all the way around and stumbled because of the unexpected lightness of the load.

"What are we throwing away? Inflated balloons?" she asked.

She could still hear her mother and aunt laughing as she walked through the narrow backyard to the alley. Both bags bobbed along with each step Becky took. She couldn't help but wonder what was in them. Her curiosity got the best of her. Next to the dumpster she carefully untwisted the plastic tie on one bag and peeked in. It was trash all right. Lots and lots of wrapping paper, plastic pop bottles, paper plates and cups, plastic forks, a happy birthday disposable tablecloth, and crumpled up napkins. Becky closed the bag. In the second bag she saw more wrapping paper, some gift boxes, and the box the cake came in. As Becky carefully retwisted the tie, she heard

Mom calling from the house. Becky hurried to the house, where her mom was putting on her raincoat. It was time to go home.

"What a trashy party!" said Becky as they got in the car.

"Becky Robinson! What a terrible thing to say!"

The surprised look on her mother's face made Becky laugh.

"No—I mean, the party was fine. But there was so much trash."

Her mother nodded her head, "Yes, and it will be the same thing at our house when all your cousins come over next month for Christmas. There will be twice as many people—and presents for everyone! And don't forget the turkey dinner. There'll be dozens of bags of trash, and you'll have to carry each and every one to the curb."

Becky knew her mom was kidding around now. But it bothered her that her mother wasn't taking her seriously.

Becky's class had been learning about their city's trash problem. Reporters talked (and wrote) about overflowing landfills, wandering trash barges, and recycling.

"I'm learning about different ways we can throw out less stuff, Mom. I bet we can have Christmas at our house with wrapped presents for everyone, and still throw out less trash than we did today. Tell you what. Let me use some of the ideas I've heard about, and if we have as much trash at our Christmas party as there was at this birthday party, I'll carry out the trash for a year." She paused, and then remembered to add, "without complaining."

"That's quite a commitment, Becky. Dad would love to hear about that! Sounds like you're growing up to be as thrifty as your Aunt Mildred. That woman never throws anything out."

Becky thought about her aunt. Yes. She'd have to be sure to get her aunt's ideas about making less trash. Aunt Millie would be a wonderful help. Already Becky was making plans. Mom's words interrupted her thoughts.

"This could be interesting, Becky, but I don't have time to deal with a lot of extra work.

Just how are you planning on pulling this off?"

"I'm not quite sure, yet. I'll need some time to make some plans. But I'll be sure to check with you about every detail as we go along, okay?"

"Okay," her mother answered hesitantly. Then she added, "Just what are you expecting if you're successful with this?"

Becky had almost forgotten about that, but it didn't take her long to answer, "If there's less trash, then can you and Dad buy me a new bike for my birthday in January?"

Becky had her fingers crossed in her lap. Her mother answered, "We'll see. I'll talk to your father."

For the rest of the ride home and into the evening, Becky was making plans. She grabbed a handful of long envelopes out of the wastebasket next to her mother's desk and made list after list.

The phone call to her aunt was a success. Aunt Millie was delighted to do all she could to help.

With a triumphant last exclamation point,

Becky finished her plans and ran down to show them to her mother. Mom was practicing the piano for the Sunday school Christmas service. Becky knew better than to interrupt. When her mother finished "Go Tell It on the Mountain," she took a look at Becky's lists.

"Not bad, Becky. Are you going to let all of our guests know about your goal? You know there will be 15 people here for dinner."

Becky pointed out that part of her plan. The Robinson's Christmas dinners were always potluck, no matter whose family hosted the celebration. "I'll make the phone calls to see what people would like to bring for the dinner," she explained. "Then I'll explain my 'waste-not' goal for this year."

Becky and Mom planned the menu. Aunt Gayle's family would bring appetizers, a cranberry salad, and punch. Aunt Millie would make homemade rolls, her incredible candied yams, and a birthday cake for Jesus for dessert. Becky and Mom and Dad would provide the turkey and stuffing, mashed potatoes, vegetables, and ice cream for the cake.

Becky jumped out of bed the next morning. It was a sunny Saturday, a perfect day to go visit her neighbor, Mrs. Williams. Mrs. Williams was the best gardener in the neighborhood. Mrs. Williams said her flowers grew because she fed them so well. When Becky asked what kind of food plants eat, Mrs. Williams took her behind her garden shed and pointed to her compost pile. It didn't look like much, just a big pile of grass clippings and brown leaves. But when Mrs. Williams turned over a shovelful of the stuff, beneath the surface it was a rich ebony color. And it was loaded with worms!

"In here are most of the nutritious goodies that plants love to eat. This is what makes my plants so beautiful," Mrs. Williams explained. "Do you know I can even bury eggshells, vegetable peels, and stale bread in here, and then in a few months it will turn into this black gold? It's called humus."

Becky thought that maybe the scraps from the Robinson Christmas dinner could go into Mrs. Williams' compost pile. Better there than into a trash bag at her house! Mrs. Williams said she would be delighted to take their scraps, as long as they were just vegetable and bread scraps, no meat.

"I'll send some flowers to your house next summer to say thank you for themselves," Mrs. Williams laughed. Becky smiled and turned to hurry back to her house. Before she headed down the sidewalk, Mrs. Williams asked, "Do you want to know how to make wrapping paper that can also go into the compost pile?"

Becky's eyes grew wide with excitement. She didn't know there was such a thing.

Mrs. Williams told her what she would need, and even helped her make a roll of paper long enough for all the presents her family would be wrapping. As Becky walked back to her own house, she could just picture herself cruising down the sidewalk on her brand-new bicycle.

The weeks passed in a hurry. Before she knew it, Becky was at the store, shopping for the groceries the family would need for the holidays.

The first thing she kept in mind was something her teacher had called *precycling*—thinking about how something is packaged before you even buy it and bring it home.

For example, carrots could be bought in one-pound bags, two-pound bags, or in no bags. You could take them loose or put them all in one reusable plastic bag. Becky filled a whole bag with carrots and used a twist tie on the bag so they'd be able to reuse it at home.

Becky and her mom picked out candy, crackers, and chips, all in the bulk food section. The most fun part of shopping was picking out the turkey. In the meat department there were turkeys everywhere. Frozen turkeys, fresh turkeys, small turkeys, big turkeys. Becky wanted to find the heaviest turkey in the store.

Mom stared at Becky and said, "Right now, I'm looking at the biggest turkey in the whole city." They decided on a plump, 24-pound bird.

A couple pounds of margarine in reusable plastic tubs, two liters of soda pop, and ice cream in a reusable plastic bucket, and Becky's shopping was complete. As they headed to the checkout stand, they pushed their cart through the paper products aisle. Mom wanted to grab some decorated paper napkins, but Becky shook her head. She and Aunt Millie would make sure there were cloth napkins for the dinner. Mrs. Robinson pointed at some red and green paper drinking cups. Again, Becky shook her head.

A shelf next to the cash register was full of red and green candles for the dinner table. Did Becky think those would be a good idea for their celebration? Becky thought for a minute and then nodded her head. They were pretty, and they wouldn't get thrown in the trash after one use.

On Christmas Eve, Mrs. Robinson had time to practice one of the choir's difficult pieces just one more time before they headed for church. Becky's two younger brothers were hurrying around upstairs, trying to find their shoes. Mr. Robinson called up to them to hurry it up. Becky finished some labels she was mak-

110

ing for the next day's cleanup crew. On the backs of five used envelopes, she had written neatly with a felt-tip marker, "Cat Scraps," "Re-Use," "To Be Recycled," "Mrs. Williams," and "Laundry."

Becky couldn't remember a year she hadn't enjoyed the drive back home from church after the Christmas Eve Sunday school service. All the buildings and streets shone with decorations. Mom could finally relax because the Sunday school service was over. And Christmas was only hours away.

As Becky went to sleep that night, she had no idea what she would find under the Christmas tree in the morning. But she knew she'd be getting a bicycle for her birthday in January.

Aunt Millie was the first to arrive the next day. She wanted to come early to help Becky. The bird was already stuffed and in the oven when Aunt Millie knocked at the door. Mrs. Robinson opened the door for her sister. They couldn't hug because Aunt Millie was loaded down with boxes and bags.

Aunt Millie started unloading her packages. The first bundles to be unpacked were presents for under the tree. Each present was wrapped in a brand new bathroom towel! All the presents for the Robinson family were wrapped in red bath towels, except for Mrs. Robinson's package. That was wrapped in a red washcloth. Probably a necklace or a pair of earrings, thought Becky. All the packages for Grandma and Aunt Gayle's family were wrapped in green linens.

Then Aunt Millie brought out a stack of extra dishtowels and rags (so they wouldn't have to use any paper towels to clean up spills and messes), and a basket of her wonderful homemade rolls. They were still warm! In the car, one last box held the sweet potato casserole and a beautiful birthday cake for Baby Jesus. Every year, before dessert, the whole family gathered around the nativity scene and sang "Happy Birthday" together. They knew that God's gift of His own Son to be their Savior was the whole reason for Christmas.

Sooner than everyone expected, the rest of

the guests arrived. Aunt Gayle set her goodies on the table, as the rest of her family spread their gifts under the tree. All of their presents were packed in reusable gift bags.

Dinner was delicious. They hurried to do the dishes so they could open presents and then have dessert. Becky was in charge of the cleanup crew. Aunt Millie took all the turkey meat off the bones right away and bagged up the meat for the refrigerator. She put the turkey bones in a kettle of water to simmer on the stove.

"Might as well start making the soup right away," she said.

By the back door Becky had put a couple grocery bags, a bucket, the cat's bowl, and a laundry basket. Each one was labeled with one of the envelopes that Becky had prepared ahead of time. Potato peels, bread scraps, and leftover vegetables went into the bucket for Mrs. Williams' compost pile. Turkey scraps from people's plates went into the cat's bowl. Cans and bottles were rinsed and put in the bag labeled for recycling. Anything that could be re-used was washed and stacked on the

table. The laundry basket held napkins, dishtowels, and rags. One bag was for trash.

"Well, you did it, Becky!" said Becky's mom. "You organized this birthday party for Jesus, and the only trash I can find are these two-liter plastic soda-pop bottles." Before Becky could remind her mom that even the pop bottles could be recycled, Aunt Millie grabbed one bottle from her mother, turned it over, and stuck it on the top of her broomstick. "I'll cover this head with newsprint, add a face and yarn hair, staple on a body cut from poster board, and this will be the dandiest—and biggest—stick puppet you've ever seen."

Uncle Gene grabbed the other pop bottle and pushed it on to the end of his mop handle. "I'll do the same. We can make Mary and Joseph puppets, shepherds and Wise Men, and add a new twist to next year's Sunday school service!"

Becky smiled as she thought about next year. "Maybe the weather will be nice enough that I'll be able to ride my new bike to next year's service," she said out loud.

"Congratulations, Kitten, you win," Mom laughed.

POP-BOTTLE PUPPET

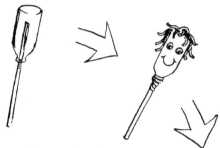

Materials
- 2-liter plastic soda-pop bottle
- Broomstick or dowel that fits snugly into the bottle opening
- Newsprint sheets
- Masking tape
- Glue
- Construction paper scraps
- Poster board
- Yarn
- Stapler
- Markers
- Scissors

Push the dowel into the bottle opening and tape. Cover bottle with newsprint. Use markers to draw a face. Add yarn for hair. Cut out a large body from poster board. Staple securely to stick.

T. Buzzards

Just as Mrs. Brown went to the kitchen door to call Kristen and Matt in for dinner, the shooting started again. As the shots rang out, huge birds flew from the trees. Mrs. Brown, Matt, and Kristen watched as the giant birds scattered from the tall trees in their neighbor's yard. Here we go again, thought Mrs. Brown.

The neighbors weren't trying to kill the birds; they didn't even want to hurt them. The idea was to scare the birds away from nesting, or even roosting, in the neighbor's trees.

The birds were gone, and all was quiet as the Browns sat down to eat dinner. The sound of gun shots rang out again as dessert was

served. This time it was another neighbor in another yard.

By now it was almost dark. The Browns knew that neither neighbor would do any shooting after dark. No, after dark they changed their tactics to scare the birds. They went in their backyards with boards and flashlights. As they shined the flashlight directly at the tired birds, they banged the boards together. Off again the birds would fly, hoping to find a quiet place to rest for the night.

The Browns and their neighbors lived in a rural area that used to be all farmland and woods. In the past 20 years, the land had slowly been developed to add many new houses. With each new development came miles of newly paved roads. Several land developers valued the woods around their new homes and encouraged wildlife to stay. They put up bluebird houses and nesting boxes for hawks and osprey. Where they flooded the land for recreational lakes for their residents, they encouraged fish populations and waterfowl. The developers only allowed boats with electric motors on their lakes, to prevent the water being contaminated with gasoline and motor oil.

With all this attention to preserving and encouraging wildlife, these big birds now circling over the woods behind the Brown's house had been overlooked. Although the strong wings of these big birds were to be admired, the birds themselves were considered ugly, smelly, dirty, and even frightening. It was hard to believe as they gracefully soared above the trees, but these birds were ugly, old turkey buzzards.

Over the past couple of years, the Browns and their neighbors watched the sightings of turkey buzzards steadily increase in their neighborhood.

One morning Mrs. Brown read an article in the newspaper about the turkey buzzard problem at a nearby housing development and what the home owners' association had been doing about it. Mrs. Brown was sickened by what she read.

Apparently the residents of Lake Majestic

had decided to deal with their turkey buzzard problem by trying to scare away the birds with noisy firecaps. They cut down the tall dead trees where the birds had built their nests, hoping to send the birds far away in search of a new nesting area. The article said that the next phase of the buzzard relocation process would be to kill one of the birds and tie the carcass to a tall tree.

Mrs. Brown sadly shook her head. These city people who were moving out to the country certainly had a lot to learn. These same people who were so offended by the presence of turkey buzzards would be even more squeamish about the idea of a large dead animal lying in the woods or along the side of the road. Didn't they realize that the turkey buzzards' job was to clean up the carrion from roadways and nearby woods? Thinking about the road reminded Mrs. Brown that the new roads that had been built for the new homes were probably the cause of the increase in buzzards. Before she could give any more thought to the dilemma of the unpopular birds, the rest of the family came downstairs ready for breakfast. Even in the Brown family, vultures and carrion were not very appetizing mealtime topics, so Mrs. Brown forgot about the birds' plight for the time being.

During breakfast the family talked about the tractor that Mr. Brown wanted to buy. He wanted to go look at it sometime today. Matt and Kristen asked if they could go along too. Mr. Brown agreed to pick them up after school, and they would go to the farm to see the tractor.

"We might make an evening of it and go out for pizza as well," he smiled. Matt and Kristen cheered.

That evening as Mrs. Brown enjoyed a quiet walk, she noticed the buzzards returning to scout out an area to spend the night. They flew in huge, lazy circles. Moving through the air like silent gliders with wingspans up to six feet, the birds' small red heads turned from left to right, apparently watching for a safe place to roost for the night. More and more birds came into sight. Mrs. Brown tried to count them; but after 53, she thought she might be counting the same birds more than once. She had never seen so many buzzards at once. It was almost frightening, but fascinating as well.

More than 30 of the huge birds had settled in the trees when a man came out of the house next door with his rifle. Some of the birds took to the air at the sight of the gun. It only took a shot or two to get the remaining birds to abandon their perches. Mrs. Brown watched as the birds searched the sky, scoping out another likely roosting area for the night. They circled above the woods and settled in the trees on the next hilltop. First, one at a time dropped down from the sky to try out the newly-selected roosting area. When it seemed safe, more and more birds settled in until there were more birds in the trees than left in the sky.

Mrs. Brown thought about the wonder of God's creation and the complete food cycle He had designed. God hadn't skipped a detail. Every creature had a purpose and place in His grand scheme.

When the shots rang out a second time,

Mrs. Brown jumped. Of course—the neighbor to the east had walked all the way out to where the birds were and sent them on their way.

It was getting a bit ridiculous, now. Neither neighbor wanted the birds in their yard, because 50 turkey buzzards resting for the night could make quite an ugly—and smelly—mess on the ground below. Mrs. Brown wondered what she would do if the birds settled in her woods. After all, Matt and Kristen often wandered in those woods after school.

As the birds continued to circle and settle again, Mrs. Brown tried to think of a plan for buzzard management. All animals need water, food, shelter, and a place to raise their young. If any of this is not available, the species will abandon the area. Mrs. Brown knew it was not possible to eliminate the birds' source of water, and nobody wanted all the trees cut down to get rid of the birds' shelter and nesting sites. The only necessity that could be increased or decreased by people would be the birds' food supply.

Mrs. Brown knew what turkey buzzards

ate, and she was thankful that there were animals like buzzards in God's plan for nature. When animals die in the woods, or are killed by a car on the highway, buzzards are one way the bodies are cleaned up and removed from the area. Mrs. Brown shook her head as she imagined what the outdoors would be like if there were no animals like buzzards to clean up. Stinky!

With all the new highways in the county, the number of animals killed by cars increased. With the increase of meat, "carrion," available for the buzzards, there was also an increase in the population of buzzards in the area. It all made sense, but the question was still unanswered. How could people reduce the amount of carrion available for the large birds, and eventually lower the number of buzzards to a tolerable amount?

Mrs. Brown had a few ideas and decided to sit down and write some letters. As Mr. Brown and Matt and Kristen came in the door full of news about the tractor, she shared her ideas with them. They were quick to join the campaign.

"Let's write a flyer and make copies to give to the neighbors," Mr. Brown suggested. "Turkey buzzards watch for mice and other rodents. People need to discourage rodents on their property."

"But we need to tell them not to use poison, Dad," Matt interrupted. "A buzzard or another animal could eat the dead mouse and get sick and die from the poison."

"That's right," Mrs. Brown agreed. "One way to cut down on rodents is to remind people to keep tight lids on their trash cans. And if they have bird feeders in their yard, they need to pick up extra bird seed from the ground."

"We need to warn people to drive carefully," Mr. Brown said, "so they don't hit animals."

"One time Becky's mom hit a deer with her car," Kristen said. "She was so frightened, and the deer was hurt. She went right home and called the police. They sent someone to help the deer."

"That's exactly what should be done," said Mr. Brown. "We need to tell people that, if they hurt an animal, they should call the police. If the animal is killed, they should call the highway department. If dead animals are taken to the Humane Society instead of being left on the road or thrown into the woods, the buzzards won't be attracted to this area."

"Well, let's get these ideas on paper and organize a letter-writing campaign," Mrs. Brown announced. She typed letters as Mr. Brown looked up addresses. Matt and Kristen addressed envelopes and licked stamps. One letter went to the Lake Majestic Homeowners' Association, two went to the newspapers, one went to each of the county's radio stations, and two went to the mayor and the county commissioners' office.

The Browns looked at their stack of letters. "Good job, everybody," Mrs. Brown smiled.

"I sure like the idea of writing letters to help keep some of the buzzards away, instead of shooting guns," Kristen said. And everyone agreed.

CREATE A FOOD-CYCLE QUILT

Materials
- Sheets of drawing paper and brightly colored construction paper
- Markers or crayons
- Tape

Draw a large, bright sun on one piece of paper. Use masking tape to tape the sun in the center of a wall or display area. Ask your family or friends to help draw pictures to add to the quilt. First draw pictures of plants that get their energy to make food directly from the sun. Include plankton, algae, grains, flowers, berries, nut trees, grasses, vines, and root vegetables. Tape these pictures around the sun.

Next tape pictures of plant-eating animals next to their plant food. Then tape pictures of predators next to these animals. Also include animals that depend on one another or on plants for reasons other than food. (For example, fish get oxygen from green plants underwater.) As the patchwork quilt grows, fill any holes with brightly colored construction paper.

After planning your design on paper, you may wish to make a real quilt with fabric squares.